P9-EDH-959

THE LUCKY CAT

THE
LUCKY
CAT

by

FRANCES AND RICHARD LOCKRIDGE

with illustrations by

ZHENYA GAY

J. B. Lippincott Company

EW YORK

Contents

THE LUCKY CAT

CHAPTER ONE

A Cat Steps Out

THE DOOR SHOULD NOT HAVE BEEN LEFT OPEN. ANY CAT will go through an open door to see what is on the other side, because any cat is sure that on the other side of any door there are new and exciting things to smell and see, and probably mice. Flutters did not think twice about it when she found the door open. She merely jumped once, and was on the other side. That is how it began.

If there had really been mice on the other side of the door, Flutters probably would have gone back into her apartment as rapidly as she had gone out of it, because Flutters was afraid of mice. She had been since she was a kitten and lived in the country. She had been afraid of mice since the first time her mother, a proud cat named Diana, had brought her a practice mouse and had explained—speaking in cat, of

3

course—that cats are expected to catch mice, and that they cannot begin too early. Flutters had taken one look at the mouse, which was very small—a kitten-size mouse, really—and had been so terrified she began to tremble. There had been quite a scene about it with her mother.

Flutters had hardly seen a mouse since. She had left the country and come to live in the city and, although there are plenty of mice in cities, and rats too, there were none in Flutters' apartment. There were people in the apartment to take care of Flutters—Mr. and Mrs. Burns and their children, Patty and Howdy. There was also a woman who came in every day to keep the apartment clean and to cook dinner for Flutters and the rest of the family.

It was this woman, the maid, who left the door open. Mr. and Mrs. Burns would have been more careful and so would Patty and Howdy. The maid should have been, but she was a new maid and hadn't learned how fast cats can move when they are in a hurry. The last thing Mrs. Burns had said that day, when she left the apartment to go shopping, was, "Now be sure you don't let the cat out," and the maid, who was named Agnes, had said she certainly would not. But then, when the delivery boy came from the grocery with a big box of things, Agnes forgot all about Flutters—not for long, but for long enough. It was just the chance Flutters had been waiting for.

What Flutters found on the other side of the door was a hall, with a polished tile floor on which, as she landed after her leap, Flutters skidded. This surprised her, because cats don't skid very often and hate to. Skidding embarrasses them. The floor also had a very strong, strange odor—it had been waxed the day before—and, indeed, the whole place she was in smelled most peculiar to Flutters. Odors a human would hardly notice, or not notice at all, are very noticeable to a cat. Flutters smelled not only the wax on the floor, and the paint on the walls, she smelled strange people, and the French poodle who lived in the other apartment on the floor and had been out walking that morning, and what the people in the other apartment had had for lunch—and for dinner the night before, for that matter—and a hot, oily odor which came from an elevator. People wouldn't have smelled any of these things, except perhaps the wax on the floor. But the odors were so strong, to a cat's nose, and so unfamiliar and confusing, that they almost knocked Flutters over.

Flutters would have been glad, at that moment, to go back into the apartment, where she knew how everything smelled. But then the grocery boy came out of the apartment and closed the door behind him and Flutters, naturally, disappeared into the recess of another doorway until he had gone by. She didn't know him, and anyway he was whistling. Flutters hated whistling; it hurt her ears. Sometimes Howdy would tease her a little, knowing how she felt about whistling, and she would jump up on his lap and put one small, brown paw over his puckered lips. But Flutters loved Howdy, as she did Patty and Mr. and Mrs. Burns, too, and knew she could do anything she wanted to with any of them. The grocery boy was different.

While she waited, Flutters looked all around her. She watched the boy go down the hall and stand in front of a door; she heard a great clattering noise (which frightened her) and then the door opened and the boy stepped through it, still whistling. He had gone into the elevator, but Flutters didn't know that. She didn't know about elevators; she had come to the apartment shut up in a black box and hadn't been out of the apartment since. She had, in fact, lived a very sheltered life up to the day the door was left open. Of course, she was only about nine months old.

She watched the boy disappear, and at the same time she looked at the door to the apartment kitchen, which was the one she had come out of. She more than half expected to have somebody she knew, Patty or Howdy probably, come out and chase her. She more than half wished someone would. It was fun to be chased, and in the end to let one's self be caught and picked up and talked to. Already, she missed the warmth and the safety of the apartment, and the voices and hands she knew. But at the same time, it was interesting where she was, and it was new. A cat gets bored with the same old things, even when they represent all a cat wants. A young cat does, especially. Flutters could have gone back to the door and scratched at it, and talked—Flutters had a voice which could be heard through any door—

and Agnes would surely have heard her and let her in. But Flutters didn't. She was afterward to wish she had.

Instead, after she had waited until she was sure the delivery boy was entirely gone, she went down the hall in the direction he had taken. She went very carefully, stopping now and then to smell new things, particularly the door of the apartment where the French poodle lived. Her dark brown tail, usually very sleek and like a whip, was fluffed a little—not really bushy, but ready to get bushy at any moment. Flutters was excited, and whenever she got excited her tail fluffed out. She stopped at the door the delivery boy had gone through, and smelled it. But then there was again the loud, clattering noise behind the door—the elevator had started up from below—and Flutters was frightened and ran. She ran around a corner and came to a flight of stairs.

When she had lived in the country, with her mother and brother and sister, and some people too, it had been in a two-story house, so the stairs did not surprise Flutters. She had not thought about stairs since, but when she saw them she instantly knew all about them, and how a cat went up and down. She went down. At first, she went as she had when she was a kitten, and not big enough to do anything but jump from one step to the one below it, and then jump again. But almost at once, she realized that now she did not need to do this. She could run down the stairs almost as she could run on level, putting each hind paw, in order, where the corresponding forepaw had just been. Cats do this without having to think about it, knowing that a place which is safe for a front paw is also safe for a back paw. You can't always be looking to see where hind feet go.

Flutters ran down a flight of stairs, stopped on a landing to look around and to smell around, and to listen with her brown, pointed ears—moving her ears backward and forward and to the sides to pick up any stray noises—and then went down another flight to another landing, and did the same thing again. She kept this up until there were no more stairs to go down. She had gone all the way to the basement of the apartment house.

She was in a noisy, smelly area, and the floor felt harsh under her feet—harsh and gritty. But it was an interesting place, full of boxes and trunks, and full of shadows. There were any number of places into which a cat could get and Flutters started to get into them, going under things, and behind things. Flutters probably would have stayed there indefinitely, and somebody would have found her and taken her back to the Burns apartment, if something hadn't happened. What happened was that Flutters smelled mouse.

She remembered the smell instantly. She laid her whiskers back along her pointed brown face, and her blue eyes got round instead of almond shaped, as they usually were, and she laid her ears back. Also her tail got bigger. And then Flutters, very carefully, backed away from the awful,

the frightening, smell of mouse. She backed until she could hardly detect the smell at all, and then she turned and ran. She was an almost grown-up cat, and she was still afraid of mice!

Running, she came to an open door, and ran through it, and down a hallway, and to another door. It was open, too. And through it, Flutters could smell the out-of-doors. It was city out-of-doors, not country. Before, Flutters had smelled it only through the open windows of the apartment, which was on the fourth floor. Flutters hesitated and then went, cautiously, through the door. She was entirely through it when she smelled dog.

And almost as soon as she smelled dog, she saw dog. It was a big dog, not fastened to a person, as dogs she had seen when she looked down from a window always were.

The dog saw Flutters at almost the same moment, and barked, in a very unpleasant way, and at the same time the hair on the back of the dog's neck, and then all along the dog's back, stood up on end.

And Flutters—well, *all* of Flutters' fur stood up, all over her body. Her tail got several times its usual size and stood straight up; her lips drew back from her sharp white teeth. She looked, standing on a step, facing the dog, as if she were being blown by a high wind. But she stood her ground. Then she began to growl and hiss. Then, her legs stiff, she began to move toward the dog.

Flutters was scared to death of mice. But she was not afraid of dogs at all. She never had been.

Of course, it has to be remembered that Flutters had, until then, led a very sheltered life indeed.

CHAPTER TWO

The Search Begins

Mrs. Burns was the first of the family to find out what had happened. She came home in the middle of the afternoon, a little tired from shopping but pleased, because she had found a spring hat she liked. She opened the door to the apartment and Flutters wasn't there—wasn't waiting just inside the door, ready to say hello.

With most cats, this wouldn't have meant anything in particular; a good many cats, however much they may like their people, don't go to the trouble of meeting them when they come home. But Flutters almost always did. She met Mrs. Burns, if Mrs. Burns had been out, and then Patty, when Patty came home from school, and, a little later in the afternoon, Howdy. Then, about five thirty, Flutters met Mr. Burns when he came home from the office. After that, things were the way Flutters liked them—everybody at home, and almost time for dinner.

Now and then, of course, she missed. No cat is perfect. Sometimes Flutters fell asleep so hard that even her large, pointed ears didn't detect the sound of someone at the door until it was too late to get there. When that happened, Flutters didn't run to try to get there on time. Flutters waited a minute or two, and then sauntered out to meet whoever had come in, pretending that nothing out of the way had happened and not admitting for a moment that she had overslept. A cat has her dignity to consider.

But this afternoon she was not at the door and she did not come sauntering out of another room. Mrs. Burns was still thinking about her new hat, and that she would like a cup of tea, so for several minutes she was only partly conscious that Flutters wasn't there—she knew something was wrong, but not precisely what it was. Then she thought, "Where's Flutters?" and said, "Flutters? Come here, Flutters."

Flutters didn't come, of course. But Agnes, the maid, came out of the kitchen. Agnes looked worried and unhappy; as soon as she looked at Agnes, Mrs. Burns knew something had happened.

"Mrs. Burns," Agnes said. "That cat. I've looked all over for her."

Agnes was wearing an apron, and she twisted it in her hands. Although she hadn't been with the Burnses long, she knew how they all felt about Flutters.

"Agnes!" Mrs. Burns said. "She didn't get *out!*"

"I don't see how," Agnes said. "I'm sure I never left the door open."

Agnes was sure, too. She just didn't count the time the door had been open to let the grocery boy in.

"Oh—*Agnes!*" Mrs. Burns said. She thought how terrible Patty and Howdy were going to feel. For that matter, she felt terrible herself. "*Flutters!*" Mrs. Burns said. "Where are you, Flutters?"

But Flutters, of course, couldn't hear her.

Agnes and Mrs. Burns really searched the apartment, then. It was a big apartment, and it is hard enough to find a lost cat in even a small apartment. There is practically no limit to the number of places a cat can get herself into, and end by getting shut up in—closets, of course, but also drawers and boxes and small places under things and behind things that one would never think even a small cat could wedge into. And there is always the chance that a cat may merely be hiding, just for the fun of it. If a cat is hiding, people can look for hours and not find even a purr, unless the cat wants them to.

We know Flutters wasn't in the apartment, but Mrs. Burns and Agnes didn't. They searched everywhere. Finally they were looking in places that they *knew* no cat could be, just to be looking somewhere. All the time, Mrs. Burns kept calling "Flutters. Here Flutters" and Agnes kept saying, "kitty-kitty-kitty," although that wouldn't have meant anything to Flutters, even if she could have heard it. Flutters knew her own name, and it wasn't "Kitty."

They were still looking, although really they had about given up, when Patty came home from school. Patty was twelve years old. She was blond, like her mother. She had blue eyes. The first thing she noticed when she opened the door was that Flutters wasn't there, so the first thing she said was, "Flutters. Where are you, Flutters?"

"Darling," Mrs. Burns said. "I'm awfully afraid something has happened to—" She didn't need to finish.

"Oh!" Patty said. "Oh—*Mother!*"

Patty wanted to cry, but managed not to. There wasn't time for that.

"We've looked everywhere," Mrs. Burns said. "I'm afraid she must have got out, somehow."

"No mam," Agnes said. "I don't see how. Unless she fell out a window."

Nobody had thought of that before. It was an awful thing to think. Cats can fall a good ways and not get hurt, but not out of fourth floor windows, onto cement sidewalks.

"*Agnes!*" Mrs. Burns said.

"Oh!" Patty said.

Howdy came in just at that moment, and he had to be told.

"Agnes thinks maybe she fell out—oh!" Patty said. Then she really did start to cry. She thought about all the gay things the little cat did, and how she was afraid of mice but not afraid of dogs, and about how she would run and get a wadded up piece of paper and bring it back.

"Of course she didn't," Howdy said. He was always a polite boy, especially to maids. But he turned to Agnes and his face was red and angry. "That's foolish!" he said. "She wouldn't ever fall out a window. She's a *smart* cat. She got out, somehow."

Agnes just shook her head. She seemed very certain. That made Howdy stop and think. He thought carefully and after a moment decided what could have happened.

"Look, Agnes," he said, "didn't somebody come you had to let in? Like—like the man from the cleaners?"

"Comes Wednesday," Agnes said. "This is Friday." But then, for the first time, she looked as if she weren't certain any longer.

"Somebody else," Howdy said. "It doesn't have to be the man from the cleaners. Anybody." He waited a moment. "Please think, Agnes," he said. "There must have been *some*body."

"Well," Agnes said, "the boy came from the grocery. But that cat wasn't anywhere around and I'd have seen her and—"

"I wish," Patty said, "you wouldn't go on calling Flutters 'that cat.' That's what I wish."

She was still crying a little, so the words weren't very clear.

Of course it wasn't hard, after they had heard about the grocery boy—Agnes had to admit he had come into the kitchen with a big box and left the door open—to guess what had happened. Agnes kept insisting that "that cat" couldn't have got out without being seen. But Mrs. Burns, and Patty and Howdy, knew better. They knew that a cat, particularly an intelligent cat like Flutters, can do almost anything without being seen, or heard, for that matter. It's the way cats are made; otherwise, how would they ever catch any mice?

"Come on," Howdy said to his sister. "Maybe she's still in the building. We'll *all* look."

But Agnes's feelings were hurt. Of course, it had been her fault that Flutters had got out, but her feelings were hurt just the same.

"Mrs. Burns," Agnes said, "do you want me to get dinner or look for that cat? Because I can't do both, now can I?"

"She's afraid of you anyway," Patty said. "You'd just—"

"Patty!" Mrs. Burns said, and Patty stopped. After a moment Patty said, "I'm sorry, Agnes."

"A person can't be everywhere at once," Agnes said and then, when Mrs. Burns nodded at her, went out to the kitchen. Mrs. Burns and the children looked for Flutters.

They looked on all the eight floors of the apartment house, and kept calling "Flutters. Here Flutters." Other people who lived in the house opened doors and looked out, when Howdy or Patty or their mother asked, said they hadn't seen a little cat anywhere—a little Siamese cat with brown ears and a brown tail and brown stockings up to all four of her knees; a little cat who, when she had something to say, spoke in a deep, almost harsh, voice, and not like most cats. Most cats are sopranos.

Nobody had seen Flutters from the eighth floor down to the first. The elevator men hadn't, and the doorman hadn't. They looked out into the street in front of the building and Patty walked one way to the corner and Howdy walked the other way to the other corner, both of them calling. But Flutters didn't answer. Patty still had to be careful not to cry when she called Flutters, because she kept remembering all the charming things Flutters did.

Mrs. Burns waited until they came back to the apartment house, and then said that she didn't see what more they could do, right then. She said that Dad would be home soon, and that he would think of something and—

"The basement!" Howdy said, not meaning to interrupt, but too excited by the idea to wait. "I'll bet she's down in the basement!"

The children went down the stairs at the end of a hall that opened off the first floor corridor, and Mrs. Burns waited for them.

They found a man wearing overalls in the basement—a big man, with a round, red face. He was Mr. Cummings, who came up to the apartment now and then to fix things that went wrong, like the radiators. They asked him about Flutters and described her.

"Sort of a funny looking cat?" Mr. Cummings said.

It was not the way Howdy would have described Flutters, but he said yes, he guessed so.

"Well, I'll tell you," Mr. Cummings said. "I did see a funny looking cat maybe an hour ago."

"Oh!" Patty said. "Where, Mr. Cummings?"

"Going over the fence out back," Mr. Cummings said. "Dog was chasing it."

CHAPTER THREE

Flutters Finds
a Fence

FLUTTERS HAD NOT REALLY GONE OVER THE FENCE, AS MR.
Cummings thought. She had gone to the top of the fence,
one jump ahead of the dog. She had stopped there, clinging
to the top of the fence with all her claws. Just about every
hair on her was standing straight up, and so was her bushy
tail. Her brown ears were laid back flat against her head
and, once she was on the top of the fence, she leaned down
a little and hissed and growled at the dog. The dog jumped
up and down against the fence, hitting it and bouncing
back. All the time he jumped he barked.

It had been a close thing, and Flutters knew it. She had
to change her ideas about dogs. This wasn't one of the
country dogs she had known, and sometimes chased, when
she was a small kitten. This was a different kind of dog—

a city dog. Country dogs, particularly if they live on farms, get used to cats. If they chase them at all, they're careful not to get too close; no dog wants to get all scratched up. City dogs, who usually go around fastened to people, don't learn much about cats. The dog who chased Flutters had never had a real chance to chase a cat before, and really tried to catch her. He almost did.

Flutters, crouching on top of the fence, was furious. She was also frightened. So she growled and hissed and trembled, all at the same time. And she wished—how she wished! —that Patty or Howdy or Mr. and Mrs. Burns would come and get her. She would even have been glad to see Agnes.

The dog got tired after about ten minutes, or perhaps he finally realized he couldn't ever jump high enough to reach the little cat. Flutters had had no trouble at all going up the board fence, although it was about eight feet high; she had jumped against it and then, instead of bouncing back the way the dog did, she had gone right on to the top. She knew how to do this without anybody telling her. Of course, she didn't tell the dog how to do it. She didn't talk dog anyway, and certainly didn't want to.

The dog went off to do something else, finally. Still, for almost half an hour, Flutters sat on the fence where she was. She quit growling and her fur flattened down again, and when she was sure the dog had gone, she looked down on the other side of the fence. There wasn't much to see there, except the wall of a building, almost close enough to the fence to reach out and touch. Straight down, between the building and the fence, it was dark, or would have been to a person. Flutters could see all right, of course. She saw a rat running around on the ground. Flutters shuddered, and looked the other way.

With a dog somewhere still on one side of the fence and a rat on the other, Flutters didn't, for some minutes, know what to do. Of course, she could have stayed where she was and that would have solved all her troubles—Patty and Howdy would have found her. But Flutters didn't know that; she thought she had to do something. What she did was to stand up, with all her feet bunched together, and very carefully turn around. When she had done this, she started to walk along the top of the fence. A cat can't just sit still, doing nothing, forever.

She was still being very careful—not of falling, she knew she wouldn't fall, but of all the strange things around her. Everything was strange, of course—the noises and the smells, and the things she could see. She went along the top of the fence on tip-toe, looking around in every direction and, now that she had started to explore the world, her tail bushed up again, not fully, but quite a good deal.

She went down the fence to a place where it joined another fence, which was a few feet lower. She jumped down and began to walk along the top of the new fence, although something told her that all the time she was getting farther away from home. She wanted to go home, and at the same time—now that the dog wasn't threatening her any more—wanted to stay out and see the world for a while. She felt as she had when she went through the door; she wanted to see new things, and go new places.

She walked along the new fence, looking down first on one side and then on the other. She looked down into the back yards of the buildings which, on either side, faced away from her. Some of the yards had been turned into gardens, or people had tried to turn them into gardens. A man was working in one of the gardens, scratching a little strip of earth. (He was looking for some daffodils he had planted the fall before, and which hadn't come up.) He didn't see Flutters, although she saw him. When she saw him, and realized he wasn't anybody she knew, she hurried past. Flutters didn't like strangers.

Every fence in the world comes to an end somewhere. The one Flutters was on ran the length of a city block, and she had started about half way along it. So, in time, she came to the place it ended. There was another fence at right angles to it, there, and beyond was a sidewalk and a street, with a few city trees growing just inside the curb. Flutters came to the intersection and stopped, and then she started to sit down and think it over. But she didn't.

The reason she didn't was that, coming from her right, she heard the voice of another cat. She turned instantly, and there *was* another cat—a big, black cat, with one ear chewed. He had yellow eyes, and there seemed to be a little fire burning behind each eye. He spoke again, and he had a harsh, angry voice.

Only another cat would know precisely what he said, since, of course, he spoke in cat. What he said, however, was about, "What are you doing on my fence?" Then he added something else; something unpleasant. Probably he made a remark about Flutters' appearance; perhaps he ridiculed her blue eyes.

Flutters understood him instantly, although he had a very pronounced accent. All cats all over the world understand one another, since they speak the same language, although their accents vary. Flutters' accent, for example, was Siamese, yet the black cat understood her with no trouble when she said, in her deep, hoarse voice, "It's as much my fence as it is yours. Ar-cough-OO!" The last is swearing, in cat, and will not be translated.

Of course, it wasn't as much Flutters' fence as the black cat's fence. He spent a great deal of time on it, since he did not have any settled residence, and when other cats appeared he chased them off, or tried to. When he heard her remark, he laid his ears back, and said something dreadful. Not only was she on his fence; he didn't like her anyway.

This was not because she was a different race of cat, being Siamese. Cats didn't care about things like that, one way or another. Black cats and white cats and yellow cats, and cats with creamed-coffee bodies and brown faces and ears, and brown stockings, and cats of all colors mixed together—cats don't care about things like that, or about the accents in which the cat speaks. The plain fact is that, when they first meet, no cat likes another cat. Sometimes they get to be friends, but they never are at first, and they are not very polite about showing how they feel. The black cat didn't like Flutters, and she didn't like him. Not for a moment.

He didn't give her much chance. He jumped at her. Everything was jumping at Flutters that Friday afternoon.

As he jumped, she saw how big he was; he was really a very big cat. She saw that the fire behind his yellow eyes flared up. (There were little spots of red in her own eyes, as a matter of fact, but the black cat didn't pay much attention to them.) He was a big cat, and he hadn't led a sheltered life; not at all. Flutters realized all this, and turned around and ran. He ran after her.

And instantly, Flutters knew she wasn't going to get away, unless a miracle happened. He was bigger and he could run faster, and also he was more used to running on fences. Every time he jumped, he gained. Flutters' heart beat furiously, and it wasn't only because she was running as hard as she could. She knew she was running for her life.

And she saw that she didn't have far to run. The fence ended a few feet ahead of her, and it ended in a brick wall— a wall that not even a cat could climb.

A person caught in that sort of predicament would have to stop and think, because people have to do all their thinking with their minds. Cats think with their minds, too, but they

also think with their nerves and muscles; sometimes one would think they thought with all the millions of hairs which make up their glossy coats.

So Flutters didn't stop to think what to do. She did it and thought afterward.

Without stopping, she threw herself out into the air. She seemed to lie flat on the air; almost to sail on it like an airplane. And she landed in one of the trees on the other side of the sidewalk. And she clung to the tree.

It was a tremendous leap for a little cat, and if she had had time to stop and think she wouldn't have tried it. But she didn't have time to stop and think.

The black cat wasn't being chased by anybody, so he did have time to stop and think. He realized he could make the leap if Flutters could. But he decided not to.

He just sat on the fence and told Flutters what he thought of her. He said, "Not my fence, huh? Who says it's not my fence?"

Flutters didn't. She didn't say anything. She just held onto the tree.

CHAPTER FOUR

"Lost: One Siamese Cat"

AT THE START, THEY WERE ONLY ABOUT AN HOUR BEHIND Flutters. Flutters got out a little after two o'clock in the afternoon, and it was not quite three when Mrs. Burns came home and began to look for her. At that time, Flutters was still in the basement, looking behind some boxes. The trouble was that nobody knew that, except Flutters herself, and at that moment Flutters was having a very interesting time, hadn't been chased by anything, and didn't particularly want to go home. Still, if Mrs. Burns had gone down to the basement and called, Flutters would have answered and gone back to the apartment she let the Burnses share with her. There was no way for Mrs. Burns to know that.

And when Mrs. Burns and Patty and Howdy were looking all through the apartment building, and asking every-

body if they had seen a little Siamese cat, Flutters was sitting
on the fence, wondering what to do next. Patty and Howdy
were actually on their way to the basement when Flutters
finally made her mind up and went off.

When Mr. Cummings told the children what he had seen,
they ran out into the back yard at once, and began to call
Flutters, and then she was only about half way to the end of
the fence—was just passing the man who was looking for
daffodils. If the wind had been in the other direction, it
would have carried Patty's voice to Flutters or, anyway,
Howdy's. It was as close as that, just then.

But the wind *was* in the wrong direction, and the fence
was too high for anyone to climb, except a cat. Or perhaps
a monkey. It was too high for a boy, and it would have been
too high for a good many grown men. So when Patty and
Howdy looked, they saw only a blank board fence, with no
cat on it. And when they called, no cat answered. There
was nothing for them to do in the end but to go back into
the apartment building, and hope Flutters—if the cat Mr.
Cummings had seen really *was* Flutters—had got away from
the dog.

"*Course* she did," Howdy said, with more emphasis than
he would have used if he had really been sure. "She's a smart
cat."

Nobody would argue with him about that, least of all
Patty, who knew Flutters was a smart cat. But, all the same,
Flutters was a very small cat. Maybe, she thought, the dog

had gone over the fence after Flutters. Maybe he was a smart dog. Maybe he had caught her.

"I'd like to see any old dog that could catch her," Howdy said, as they went back into the basement. But he said it mostly to keep his courage up. A dog who could catch his cat was the last thing Howdy wanted to see.

"Didn't find her, eh?" Mr. Cummings said, when they got back into the basement.

"N-no," Patty said, wanting to cry again. "Was it a big dog, Mr. Cummings?" Mr. Cummings said it was just a medium-size dog. Then he said, "That cat I saw was a mighty *little* cat." This only made Patty and Howdy surer the cat had been Flutters. They went back upstairs in the elevator. "There's no use crying about it," Howdy said.

"I'm not crying," Patty said. "Anyway, you don't care." She really was crying, of course, or almost crying.

"Like fun you're not," Howdy said. "And she's as much my cat as she is yours, any day."

He talked that way partly because he wanted to cry too but, being a boy, and older than his sister anyway, couldn't let himself.

When they got to the apartment, their father was there, and already knew about Flutters. Mrs. Burns had called him up at his office and told him, and he had come home a little earlier than he would have normally. Patty and Howdy told him what they had found out. Howdy said, "Look, Dad, I guess she got away all right, don't you?"

"Sure she did," Mr. Burns said.

"Don't cry, Patty," Mrs. Burns said. "She'll be all right."

But neither Mr. nor Mrs. Burns was really sure, whatever they said. Flutters was a very small cat, and she was out in a very big city. Also, which neither of them said, she was a valuable cat in the sense that, because she was a thoroughbred Siamese, with a pedigree, people would pay money for her. This didn't make any difference in the way the Burnses felt about Flutters, of course, but all the same it was something which had to be considered. Finding Flutters would be, to some people, like finding a pocketbook.

It was partly because he realized that some people might just keep Flutters, if they found her and knew enough about cats to know she was valuable, that Mr. Burns put an advertisement in one of the newspapers. He said that probably Flutters would come home, all right, but that they might as well be on the safe side. So he telephoned and dictated a want-ad. It read:

"Lost. Young Siamese cat, seal-point female. Answers to the name of Flutters. Reward."

Mr. Burns gave their address and telephone number.

Then he and the children went out to look for Flutters again. Since she had last been seen going over a fence, they went to look in the street on the other side of the fence—that is, they went around the block. They went first north along the street they lived in, and then east and then south along the next street. All the time they called Flutters, and they asked people—the policeman on the corner, janitors, people who lived in the houses on the other street, boys and girls who were playing in the other street. Nobody had seen a little Siamese cat. Almost nobody, for that matter, admitted knowing what a Siamese cat looked like.

It was too bad that Mr. Burns and the children didn't go around the block the other way—that is, south in their own street first, and *then* east. If they had, they would have passed under the tree Flutters had landed in while Flutters was still in it. They were that close to finding her, then.

She would have been delighted. The one thing she wanted by that time was to go home.

CHAPTER FIVE

Flutters and the Monsters

THE TROUBLE WAS THAT, BY THE TME THE ONLY THING Flutters wanted was to go home, she didn't any longer know how to get there. This can happen to cats, just as it can to anyone else. Cats can get completely lost, and this is particularly true when they are in cities.

A good many people don't know this, and believe that a cat can always find his way home, no matter how far away he gets or what confusing things happen to him. Country cats often can, and nobody know quite how they do it. Perhaps they remember everything they see and smell when they are going away from home, and use what they have seen and smelled as a guide in getting back. Perhaps they have built-in compasses, or something that works for a cat like radar.

But cities are different, and hard for a cat. Cities are too noisy, and too full of smells, and one stretch of paved sidewalk looks precisely like another stretch of paved sidewalk. One apartment house looks like another apartment house. And, of course, Flutters had never really seen the outside of the apartment house she lived in. She had come to it in a box, out of which she couldn't see, and she had left it over a fence, with a dog almost catching her tail. If the Burnses had lived in a house it would have been easier for Flutters, but they didn't.

And Flutters didn't like the tree she was in. It was not the kind of tree to give a cat confidence. It was a spindly little tree and, looking at it, you would have thought it couldn't really make up its mind whether to live or die. There was a circular grating around it, through which it got some water, but most of its roots were under the sidewalk and the street, finding very little to feed on. It was, in other words, a typical city tree.

Flutters didn't, of course, reason it out that way. She knew that it wasn't a big tree; the branch she was on wasn't large enough for even a small cat, and it was the biggest branch the tree had. Also, the tree kept shaking. This was because it grew beside a busy street, and a great many heavy trucks pounded by it. They shook the pavement, and so they shook the little tree. A big trailer truck almost shook Flutters out of it.

She waited until the black cat went about his business,

which was, chiefly, chasing other cats off his fence and seeing what there was to eat in garbage cans. It wasn't much of a life for a cat, but the black cat, who was used to it, found it rather interesting. He knew a warm basement he could get into, and places where there were rats and mice to eat, and several janitors fed him now and then. As city cats go, he was fairly successful. Of course, he had been living that way for several years. He was experienced.

Flutters wasn't. Everything was strange and frightening. Trucks and cars went back and forth on the street just under her little tree; the noise was terrific; the fumes from the motor exhausts made her choke and feel sick; she had got dirty in the basement of the apartment house, and on the fence, and was in a position where she couldn't wash herself —she had to use all her feet to hold on to the branch. Altogether, she was miserable. Also, she was beginning to get hungry.

Some cats, being as frightened as Flutters was, would just have stayed in the tree and waited for somebody else to do something. But Flutters, although she was little and young and inexperienced, wasn't that kind of cat. One thing her mother, who was such a proud cat she often thought herself as a tiger, had told Flutters over and over: Every cat has to learn to take care of herself, because some day she may have to. Mother cats have been telling their kittens that for hundreds of thousands of years, ever since there were cats. A few cats never learn, but Flutters—in spite of her unfortunate experience with her first mouse—believed what her mother had told her. She also figured that this was the day she had to begin.

So, after the black cat left, she began by coming down the tree. She backed down cautiously, stopping every now and then to look around in all directions. She was learning.

Everything frightened her, but, coming down the tree, she didn't see anything that was more frightening than anything else—she didn't see any dogs, or other cats, or people she didn't know. She waited several minutes before she jumped the last few feet to the sidewalk. On the sidewalk she stood with her legs braced, and her tail big and looked all around at everything. Across the street, behind a low stone wall, she saw some really substantial trees. The trees looked good to Flutters; a tree—a satisfactory tree—always looks good to a cat in trouble. But, of course, there was the street between her and the trees, and the street was full of monsters.

For a minute or two, she stood there, watching the monsters—noisy, and smelly and terrifyingly big—which were between her and the safety of the big trees. She stood close to the little tree, ready to go back up it if one of the monsters chased her. But none of them did; none of them seemed to pay any attention to her at all. So Flutters began to be less afraid of them. Whatever they were, they weren't after cats. She decided that, if she watched for the right time, she could run in between the monsters and get to the trees. After all, she could run fast.

She went to the curb and got ready to run. She started once and had to jump back, because one of the monsters which had been a safe distance away when she started, suddenly was almost on top of her. This puzzled the little cat and she looked after the monster—which was a Buick, and a Roadmaster at that—and tried to understand it. She didn't succeed, and gave it up. Then she saw another chance and this time really started.

She would have been all right except for one thing: She had no idea at all how fast motor cars, and trucks, can move. She knew how fast another animal could run—she could estimate a dog's speed, or another cat's, or a person's. (She had known, for example, that the black cat was gaining on her on the fence.) But she had no idea how to go about estimating the speed of a truck or a car. Few cats or dogs, or other four-footed animals, can. A good many people can't, for that matter.

So again a monster which should have been a long way off—which should have given her all the time she needed— was almost on top of her in an instant. She had got to the middle of the street, and beyond it, and here the monsters were coming from the other direction. That was part of it. But mostly it was a matter of speed. She saw the big truck in time to get away from it if it had been going at the speed

of a dog, or a person—as it ought to have been. Of course, it wasn't.

So—one instant it was far away, and the next it was there. It made a dreadful harsh noise at her. The driver was sounding his horn, warning Flutters. But Flutters was already running as fast as she could; faster than she had ever dreamed she could. And she knew it wasn't fast enough.

There was an awful, roaring moment when Flutters knew she wasn't going to make it. Then the truck was on her.

The little cat disappeared under it. Just at that awful instant, with the great roaring noise all around her, Flutters thought she heard someone call her name.

Perhaps it was only a dream the little cat had. But perhaps she did hear her name called; cats do hear things that humans can't. Perhaps she heard Patty calling "Flutters! Flutters!" in her high, clear young voice.

She might have. Patty and Howdy and Mr. Burns were only about half a block away. They were near the corner, and just about to turn into the street Flutters had been trying to cross. If they had been ten minutes earlier, or even five minutes, they would have been in time to see Flutters come down out of the little tree, and in time to stop her from running in among the cars and trucks—the things which were monsters to the frightened cat. But they weren't.

They didn't see Flutters anywhere. Flutters seemed to have vanished off the face of the earth.

The children didn't want to give up: they wanted to keep

on looking. But Mr. Burns insisted. They were tired, and it was almost dinner time.

The children didn't eat much dinner; for that matter, neither Mr. Burns nor Mrs. Burns was as hungry as usual. They all kept on worrying about Flutters.

And Patty kept thinking about the busy street they had walked along, and about all the cars and trucks. She kept *seeing* Flutters being run over. The food she tried to eat stuck in her throat.

CHAPTER SIX

Flutters Sleeps

in a Tree

FLUTTERS HAD NO IDEA WHAT HAD HAPPENED TO HER.
There had been all through her, like a spasm of pain, the
knowledge that she was not going to escape the monster.
There had been the dreadful noise. Then there had been
darkness and a great rushing of air which had knocked her
off her feet. She was back on her feet, hardly knowing she
had left them, so quickly did she move, and then something
brushed hard along her back. And then it was light again.

And there was Flutters, not knowing at all what had
happened, which was almost a miracle. There was Flutters,
standing in the street, with all her fur on end, her tail straight
up and her ears laid back. There was Flutters, faced in the
direction from which she had just come. And in an instant,
there wasn't Flutters at all. There was a streak of cat, going

the right way, which was toward the low stone wall and the trees. There was a streak of cat over the wall and another streak of cat up the nearest tree.

Flutters went up and up before she stopped. It seemed to her that she could never get high enough. Her heart was beating so that her whole body shook. She was panting. But still she went up the tree, went up until the monsters were far below; until, even in her terror, she realized they could not get her. She stopped then, and stretched out on a thick branch. Then she growled, deep in her throat. She was alive.

What had happened would have been clear to a person. It had been clear to the truck driver, who had seen Flutters bounce out into the street, unhurt. He had seen that in his rear vision mirror, and been relieved, because he was fond of cats. He had a cat at home.

The truck had gone over Flutters without touching her. Well, almost without touching her—the lowest part of the machinery under the truck had brushed her, and left a long streak of grease down her back. But the wheels had not touched her; that was the important thing, and the lucky thing. That was what was almost a miracle. The darkness Flutters experienced had been the darkness under the truck; the wind had been the rush of air as the truck went over her. A person would have realized all this and thought, "That was a lucky little cat."

But Flutters didn't. All she knew was that something

terrible had happened and now wasn't happening, and that she was safe far up in a tree, and able to growl at the monster which had chased her. Then, because she was growling at the monster, and because the monster had gone away, she began to believe that she had been the one who had chased the monster. She began to feel like a tiger then, as her mother always had. That meant she was growing up, because all grown cats have moments when they feel that they are really tigers.

The feeling didn't last, of course. After a few minutes, Flutters' fur began to lie flat again and she quit growling and was just a small Siamese cat too far up in a tall tree. She looked down and, while the height didn't make her dizzy, as it would have some people, she did wish she hadn't climbed up quite so far. She wished she were home again. Then she began to get hungry. She thought of the chopped raw meat she always had at about this time, with perhaps a few morsels of roast lamb as a special treat. She thought of the warm cushions of the sofa where she wasn't supposed to sleep, and always did. She thought of Patty's fingers stroking her along her jaw bones, gently, and rubbing gently behind her pointed ears. She thought of Mrs. Burns's lap.

And she started to go down the tree. She backed along the branch she was on until she came to the trunk, which was enormous, and then back down it. Cats always back down trees; and one can see the reason by looking at their claws, which are curved, like little sickles. A cat who tried

to go down a tree head foremost wouldn't be any better equipped than a person. So Flutters backed. She backed to another branch and rested for a few minutes, and looked down again—and realized, again, that she had climbed a very long way up. Then she backed down to another branch, and then to another.

But when she got about twenty feet above the ground, and onto a branch which was the biggest yet, she stopped and laid her ears back. The monsters out in the street were very close again, and the noise they made was very loud. Seeing them, and hearing them, brought back to the little cat that awful moment when one of them had caught her, and she began to tremble. She just couldn't make herself go any farther down the tree; she wanted to, but she couldn't.

Even when she got hungrier and hungrier she couldn't force herself to go on down the tree and try to find her way home. Even when it got cooler as evening came—and this was in April, when the evenings can get pretty cool—she stayed in the tree. Even when it began to rain she stayed there, shaking herself to try to shake off the wet. She was miserable and homesick and hungry, but she couldn't go down among the monsters. Finally, she stretched out on the branch and managed to doze a little, and to dream. She would dream she was home with the people she loved, and in the place she loved. But then she would dream about the dog, and the black cat, and then about the monster. When she dreamed of home, she purred in her sleep. When she dreamed of the monster, her whole body twitched, as if she were running.

Flutters didn't sleep well, in the strange tree, and Patty Burns didn't sleep well either, although she was in her own bed. They all looked for Flutters again after dinner. They went down into the basement, thinking she might have come back there and then, after it was dark, they went around the block again, calling. They saw several cats, but none of them was Flutters. One was the big black cat who had chased her, and he glared at them from a fence. He could have told them about Flutters, if he had been able to speak English and, of course, if he had wanted to. Probably, being the kind of cat he was, he wouldn't have wanted to.

But then Mr. Burns said there was nothing more to do until morning. They would look for her again in the morning. Since it was Saturday and neither Patty nor Howdy had to go to school, they could spend most of the day looking for her. And perhaps somebody would see the advertisement in the newspaper and bring her back.

They had been going to drive out to the country to visit the children's Uncle Charles and Aunt Margaret, and Diana, who was Flutters' mother and lived with Mr. and Mrs. Wilson. Mrs. Wilson was Mrs. Burns's sister. They had been looking forward to it, especially as Diana had some new kittens to show them, but now, of course, they couldn't go. Not with Flutters lost. The first thing in the morning, Mr.

and Mrs. Burns promised, they would start looking for her again. They would look for her until they found her. Patty and Howdy had to be content with that. They would have liked to look all night, but their father and mother said, "No."

Patty lay awake for what seemed a long time, worrying about Flutters. When she did fall asleep she dreamed about Flutters. She dreamed terrible things—that the dog had got Flutters and that Flutters had been run over and then that Flutters, not hurt at all, was shut out of the apartment house and was down at the door, alone, crying to be let in. This last dream was so real that it woke Patty up and she went to a window and opened it and listened, trying to hear Flutters crying on the street far below. She heard city sounds, people talking as they walked along and cars passing, but not Flutters.

She went back to bed and this time dreamed that Flutters was not lost at all, but had come into her bedroom and got up on the bed and curled up on it, purring. Flutters did this whenever she got the chance, although she was not supposed to. This dream, like the one about Flutters crying in front of the building, was so real that it woke Patty again. Patty said, "Flutters?" She was almost sure, for a moment, that she really did see the little cat. But what she thought was Flutters was only a fold in the comforter. It had just been another dream.

Both Patty and Howdy woke up early that Saturday

morning and it seemed forever before breakfast was ready
and eaten and they could go out again to look for Flutters.
It was a bright morning, which made everything seem more
promising, and the advertisement was in the morning paper—
"Lost: Young Siamese cat." It wasn't a very large advertisement; Howdy and Patty would have been happier if their
father had bought a whole page in the paper, so that everybody would know Flutters was lost and would help look for
her. But they realized that that would have cost too much
money. Probably a good many people would see even the
small advertisement. Perhaps, Howdy said at breakfast,
somebody had already seen it and was getting ready to bring
Flutters home.

CHAPTER SEVEN

Flutters Finds a Friend

NOBODY HAD, BECAUSE FLUTTERS WAS STILL IN HER TREE. She was awake and hungry and cold; she hadn't slept very well. She was a miserable little cat.

Most of all, she was hungry. She had had no dinner the night before, of course, and now she had no breakfast. She kept thinking of food and when she did she licked her chops with her long, pink tongue. Normally, she would have talked about how hungry she was—sometimes when she was hungry she really yelled about it. But now she knew that talking wouldn't do any good, because there was nobody to talk to.

The monsters were still going back and forth in the street under her tree, and they still frightened her. But none of them had shown any signs of chasing her up the tree and, so

far as she could see, none of them was paying any attention
to her at all. All the same, she lay on the branch for almost
two hours after it was daylight and watched the monsters
before she got up courage enough to go down. She jumped
the last several feet to the ground and, when she was on it,
she ran at once. She ran, of course, away from the monsters.

Where she was seemed strange to Flutters and yet, in a
way, it seemed familiar too. It felt as if she were in the
country again, where she had been as a kitten. She remembered about that in a way cats remember, which is hard to
describe, because it is not the way people remember. Now
that she was running on grass again it was, to her, as if she
had always been running on grass. She didn't have to think
about it and say to herself, "This green stuff is grass. I remember it from a long time ago." She just *felt* it was grass.

She was in a park. It wasn't a very big park; it was about
two blocks long and only a block wide, but to Flutters there
was a lot of it. Of course, Flutters was a very small cat. She
ran this way and that over the grass, looking for Patty and
Howdy, and for food. The grass was wet from the rain of
the night before. After a time she jumped up on what she
thought was a sofa just like the one she had at home. It was
not; it wasn't soft and comfortable. It was hard and cold. It
was dry, though, and she sat on the park bench in the sun
and began to wash up. She washed and washed. She
worked particularly hard at the streak of grease on her back.
It was a difficult place to reach with her tongue, and the

grease tasted awful. She would lick at it, reaching her head back over her right shoulder and then over her left, and stop and make a kind of face because of the awful taste. But then she would lick at it again. It didn't come off very well, but she did what she could.

She also washed all four feet, and her tail, of course. A tail is almost the most important thing there is to wash. She washed her chest, her head going up and down in a bobbing motion. After she had finished she still didn't feel very well, but she felt better. There's nothing like a good wash, if you're a cat. Also, the sun was warm. Now that she was clean, except for the streak of grease, and reasonably warm, she had plenty of time to think how hungry she was. She smelled all around for food. She did this by turning her head first in one direction and then in the other, and sniffing as hard as she could. When she did this, her nose wiggled. And, sure enough, she smelled food.

She didn't smell fresh meat, or fish, and certainly not roast lamb. But she smelled something, and went toward the smell. It was strongest when she got to a wire basket; the food was in there and Flutters knew that she had, simply *had*, to get to it. But at first she couldn't see how. She went all around the basket—which was a park trash basket, mostly filled with old newspapers and things like that—trying to find a way in. She stood up on her hind legs, and could just reach the top of the basket with her forepaws. And then she saw the food.

It was only a piece of frankfurter roll which somebody had thrown away after eating the frankfurter. Probably the roll had been bigger than the hot dog; the hot dogs people sell in parks are pretty small, sometimes. Anyway, there the end of the roll was. It wasn't anything Flutters would have given a second thought to, ordinarily, but this wasn't an ordinary morning. A lost cat has to eat what she can find.

Flutters stood on her hind legs for longer than a minute, looking at the piece of roll. Then she got down, and backed up a little, and crouched. She had very long, powerful hind legs for such a small cat. They were really longer than her front legs. Siamese cats are shaped that way, usually. Nobody knows how it happened. It makes them the best jumping cats there are.

Flutters crouched and got ready. She made sure her hind feet were on something solid. She wriggled all her muscles, to make sure they were working properly. Then she jumped. She jumped right into the basket, which was only half full of paper and things. She found the roll and began to eat it. It was hard to do anything in the basket, because the loose papers kept sinking under her. But Flutters managed. The roll, although it wasn't really anything a cat likes, tasted fine.

She was so busy with the roll that she didn't see the boys at first. If she had seen them in time, things might have worked out differently.

The boys were all about twelve. One of them was named Tim, and the others were named Roy and George and Leonard. Since it was Saturday, and they didn't have to go to school, they were on their way to play ball on the diamond at the far end of the park. They were feeling good because it was spring, and the rain had stopped and, of course, because it was Saturday. Roy saw Flutters first and stopped and pointed at her and said, "Hey, look!" They all looked. "It's just a cat," George said, after he had looked.

Flutters heard them. She looked up from the roll she was eating.

"It's a funny looking cat," Roy said. It was Leonard, who was called Lenny by everyone, who said, "Let's catch it."

Lenny didn't particularly want to hurt Flutters. He just didn't think about it, one way or another. He didn't have anything against cats. Flutters was just something to chase. So Lenny and George and Roy began to run toward the cat in the basket and, after a minute, Tim ran too. They began to yell at Flutters.

Flutters jumped, then. She couldn't get a good start on the loose paper, and she didn't have time to get ready, so she didn't jump as well as usual. She got to the top edge of the basket and then had to scramble over. By the time she got to the ground, the boys were all around her.

They didn't mean to hurt her. They just wanted to catch her. But Flutters didn't know that. She didn't know what they wanted to do. They were strange and noisy, and she had been in a lot of trouble already. This was just more trouble.

She ran one way, and Roy grabbed at her and almost caught her. She ran another and George got one hand on her, trying to hold her down. She was frightened and George, because he didn't know much about cats, and was trying to grab her fast anyway, was rough. So Flutters turned around and hissed and clawed at George's hands. Her sharp claws went in deep, and she pulled them along the hand. George said, "Ow!" and let her go. He looked at his hand. It was bleeding.

That made him mad, of course. He tried to kick Flutters, and just missed her. She ran another way and this time it was Lenny who grabbed her. She ran right into Lenny, as a matter of fact. He grabbed her with both hands. She bit Lenny. She was terrified and angry, and he hurt her. Just then she would have bitten anybody, except, of course, any of the Burnses. Anybody who is rough with a cat can expect the cat to be rough right back, which is a perfectly natural way for a cat to behave. All the same, it hurts to be scratched or bitten by a cat. When a cat bites a person, it is difficult for a person to see the cat's side of it. Neither Lenny nor George could.

"I'll teach that cat!" Lenny said, and started to tighten his fingers on Flutters' throat. Nobody knows how far he would have gone—or what Flutters would have managed to do about it, for that matter.

"Don't hurt that cat!" Tim said. He hadn't expected to

say it. He just couldn't help himself. "You leave that cat alone!" he said, then.

"Huh!" Lenny said. "Whose cat is it?" There wasn't any answer to that, because nobody knew. It was just something Lenny said, because at first he was surprised by Tim's attitude and couldn't think of anything better. Then he said, "It bit me." This was certainly more to the point, because Flutters had.

"You hurt it," Tim said. "Give it to me."

At first, Lenny wasn't going to. But he looked at Tim's face, and he remembered that Tim was the best fighter of any of them, when he had to be, and also that Tim was the pitcher on the ball team.

"Aw," Lenny said, "who wants the old cat?"

He gave Flutters to Tim, holding her out so she dangled. Flutters hissed and tried at first to scratch Tim. But he took hold of her gently. He didn't take hold of her in the best way—there are good ways to take hold of a cat and bad—but he was gentle. Flutters could tell he didn't mean to hurt her. She was still terrified, but she didn't try to scratch. She just trembled in Tim's arms.

"It's all right, kitty," Tim said. "Nobody's going to hurt you."

Flutters didn't understand what he said. She didn't even know that "kitty" meant her. *Her* name was Flutters. But the voice was all right. It was the kind of voice a cat likes—

not loud, or harsh. So Flutters licked one of Tim's hands.

"Look," Roy said, "we going to play ball? Or we going to stay here all day with this old cat?"

Tim wanted to play ball. But after Flutters licked his hand he couldn't, somehow.

"I'm going to do something about this cat," Tim said. Then, mostly because he didn't want to seem sissy, he said, "Maybe there's a *re*ward."

Nobody had thought of that before.

"Aw," Lenny said. "Who'd pay a *re*ward for a funny lookin' old cat?"

CHAPTER EIGHT

The Burnses Find Some Other Cats

PATTY AND HOWDY AND THEIR FATHER LOOKED ALMOST everywhere else that morning before they looked in the park. Of course, if they had looked there first, they might have found Flutters before Tim and the other boys did—and would Flutters have been glad! But they had no way of knowing that. The most likely place for Flutters to be, still seemed to them the square block they lived in and so, of course, they looked there first. They had looked there before, but the very place a cat isn't the first time you look for her is often the place she *is* the second time. Everybody who has ever tried to find a cat knows that.

They took longer that Saturday morning than they had the evening before, and asked more people. They looked for blocks around. They asked everybody they met and, at one time or another, they saw a good many cats. They even saw one Siamese cat, but he was walking on a leash with the lady who owned him. He looked very mad about it, but he was walking. Nobody had seen Flutters.

It wasn't until almost noon that they got around to the park. By that time the ball game was over. None of the boys who might have told them about Flutters was around and neither, of course, was Flutters. Howdy and Patty and Mr. Burns didn't know it, but they were getting further and further behind Flutters all the time.

While they were doing this, Mrs. Burns was answering the telephone and the doorbell. Plenty of people had read the advertisement in the newspaper, all right. Some of them hadn't read it very carefully, or didn't know what a Siamese cat looked like, but that didn't stop them. It was hard to believe how many people had found cats who *weren't* Flutters. Most of them telephoned, but some of them just brought the cats around.

Mrs. Burns would answer the telephone and somebody would tell her about a cat. It would be a black cat with white spots, or a yellow cat, but the person who called would be sure it was Flutters. You would think anybody would know a black cat wasn't a Siamese, but a lot of people don't, as Mrs. Burns found out.

She would explain that a black cat, or a yellow cat, couldn't possibly be Flutters, and thank the person who had telephoned, and then the doorbell would ring. There would be a little girl there with a white kitten, and the little girl would say, "I brought your cat home." Mrs. Burns would say it was a beautiful kitten, but that it wasn't their cat. She would give the little girl a cookie—and a dime, perhaps—and then the telephone would ring again. This time it would be somebody who had found a tiger cat he or she was sure was Flutters. Mrs. Burns would take care of that, and sit down to have a look at the newspaper, and the doorbell would ring. It would be a man with a tortoise-shell cat. And after he had gone, there would be somebody else on the telephone. Several of the people who called up didn't even think they had found Flutters. They thought that Mr. and Mrs. Burns, because they had lost their cat, might like to adopt one, or perhaps two or three, of the five or six kittens their cat had just had. Mrs. Burns had never realized how many cats there are in the world.

The telephone calls were still going on when Patty and Howdy and their father came home. Mrs. Burns had only to look at them to know they hadn't found Flutters, or even found out anything about her. Mr. Burns looked at his wife over the heads of Patty and Howdy, and shook his own head, in a hopeless kind of way. He didn't want to say so, but he was afraid they weren't going to find Flutters, ever. He didn't have to say so, but he was afraid something had happened to Flutters.

Mr. and Mrs. Burns took the children out to lunch, partly hoping that it would take their minds off Flutters and partly, it has to be admitted, to get away from the telephone for a while. They walked to a place a few blocks away, but all the time they were walking they were looking for Flutters and when they got to the restaurant Patty wasn't very hungry. Every time she started to eat something, she wondered if Flutters was getting anything to eat. Howdy wasn't very hungry either, but he pretended he was.

They looked some more that afternoon after lunch, and Mr. Burns called the American Society for the Prevention of Cruelty to Animals and the local Humane Society and told them about Flutters, so they would know who she was if somebody who hadn't seen the advertisement brought her in. A good many more people called up about cats which weren't Flutters, and two more brought cats to the apartment. They were nice cats—one had a face with white patches which made him look like a clown and the other was a lovely soft gray cat with big yellow eyes. It only made things worse, of course, to see cats who weren't Flutters. It made you remember how nice cats were.

They didn't find Flutters that day, or the next, although they kept on looking. They didn't look quite as hard on Sunday. It wasn't because they weren't as anxious as ever to find Flutters, and didn't miss her as much. It was because they had looked every place they could think of and were beginning to get discouraged. Patty and Howdy were still sure they would find Flutters eventually, but Mr. and Mrs. Burns, to be honest, weren't. Grown people get discouraged rather easily, sometimes. Mr. and Mrs. Burns even talked about getting a new cat—one of Diana's new kittens—if in the end they had to give up hope of finding Flutters. They didn't say anything to Howdy or Patty about that, but they talked about it between themselves.

But even when they did, they knew that no other cat would ever be like Flutters. No two cats are ever alike, no matter how much alike they look. After a time, if they had to get another cat, they would get fond of her. But she wouldn't be Flutters.

Flutters was the first cat the Burnses had ever had, you see. There is something special about a first cat.

They didn't find Flutters Monday, either. The children had to go to school and couldn't keep on looking for her. Mr. Burns had to go to his office. Mrs. Burns had to order groceries and see that the laundry went out. People have to go on doing the ordinary things, even if they have lost their cat.

And cats have to go on doing the things cats do, even when they have lost their people. It's just as bad for cats.

CHAPTER NINE

Flutters Is Taken In

THE FIRST THING FLUTTERS HAD TO DO WHEN TIM—WHOSE full name was Timothy Anderson—took her home on Saturday morning was to smell everything. She did this, of course, before she would even notice the milk Tim gave her, and which she drank only because she was very thirsty. Like most grown-up, or almost grown-up, cats, Flutters didn't care particularly for milk. Cream, yes; milk, no. Milk is for kittens.

The apartment to which Tim took Flutters wasn't much like the one the Burnses had. You could hardly call it an apartment at all. It was one room, without much furniture in it. There was a gas plate behind a curtain at one end. There were a few shelves with cans on them above the stove. The milk was out on the window sill, because there wasn't

64

any refrigerator. Tim had a cot and his father had a cot. That was about all they had. There were just the two of them; Tim's mother was dead. They were poor; very poor.

Tim's father had been wounded in the war, so that his right arm and hand were stiff. Before the war he had played a violin in an orchestra, and that was the thing he really knew how to do. With his right arm the way it was, he couldn't play any more. He had learned to write with his left hand, and then had gone to night school and learned to keep books. But he hadn't been able to get a job keeping books so he did whatever he could find to do. You might have thought that Flutters, who had lived in comfortable places all her life, would have turned up her small black nose at the place Tim took her to.

But Flutters wasn't like that. Most cats aren't, whatever people who do not understand them say. Oh, there may be a few cats, elderly cats who have been spoiled all their lives, who care a lot about soft places to sleep and carpets to walk on, but most cats don't care much. They'd rather have things like that, of course. Any cat likes to be comfortable. But what they really care about is people. What Flutters missed wasn't the Burns's big apartment. It was Mr. and Mrs. Burns and Howdy and, maybe most of all, Patty.

Flutters smelled around Tim's apartment to find out what it was like, and to see if the Burnses were there. They weren't. But the people who were there, or had been, she could smell very clearly. That is, she could smell Tim, who was there, and his father, who wasn't when Tim first brought her home. Both of them smelled like the kind of people cats like. What that smell is, nobody but a cat knows. But all cats do know. That is why, when a cat meets a person, the first thing the cat does is to smell the person's fingers. Flutters had smelled Tim's fingers before anything else, and then she wasn't afraid any more.

She examined everything in the room, and Tim sat down in a chair and watched her. He'd never really watched a cat before. She moved very carefully. She seemed to be on tiptoe. Her tail stuck straight out behind her, and it was a little bushy. She waved it from side to side. Once she seemed to smell something exciting, and her tail got bigger and she smelled in that particular place very carefully, although to Tim it looked like any other place. (A mouse had a nest there, under the floor and out of sight. But Tim, of course, didn't know that.) And once Flutters heard something, or saw something—Tim couldn't tell which—and jumped sidewise very quickly—so quickly it was all over almost before it started. Then, as if nothing had happened at all, she went under Tim's cot and smelled and looked around there. Then she came out.

She had attended to the room. Now she walked over to a place directly in front of Tim and sat down facing him. She curled her long dark tail around her body so that the tip of it rested over her forepaws, which were very precisely together. Then she opened her slanting blue eyes as widely as

she could and looked at Tim. She didn't say anything. She didn't blink her eyes. She didn't move her tail. She just looked.

Tim had never been looked at by a cat before, and being thoroughly looked at by a cat can be disconcerting. At first you think the cat must be trying to tell you something and you try to understand what it is. Then, as the cat keeps on looking, and doesn't move, or even blink, you get to feeling that there must be something wrong with you. Perhaps there is a smudge on your face. Perhaps you have suddenly turned green. At this point, some people get up and go look in a mirror, just to be sure, even when they have just washed their faces.

And then, when a cat looks at you long enough, you begin to think the cat is looking right through you. It's almost as if you weren't there at all, and this can be very upsetting. You begin almost to wonder whether you *are* there, and at this point some people pinch themselves to be sure they are.

So far as anybody knows, cats don't plan to make people feel this way. They merely want to be sure what people look like.

Sometimes it happens, when a cat looks long enough, that the person being looked at begins to feel that he belongs to the cat. People do belong to cats, of course, just as much as cats belong to people. Tim began to feel that way, and as if he ought to say something to the cat.

He didn't know precisely what to say, so he said, "Hello, kitty."

Flutters didn't say anything, then.

"What do you want, kitty?" Tim said.

This time, Flutters did answer. She spoke emphatically in her low, harsh voice, with her Siamese accent. Only another cat would have understood her. There are a good many things she may have said. She may have said, "Where's Patty?" or "Thank you for not letting me get hurt." She may merely have said, "Where's the meat?" Tim didn't know. He merely knew that he had never heard a cat talk that way, in that kind of voice, with that much emphasis. So Tim said, "You are a funny cat, aren't you?" He was just making conversation, of course.

Flutters didn't understand him, either. But she knew the tone of voice, and liked it, and, all at once, it made her dreadfully homesick. This wasn't Patty or Howdy, or anybody she knew. But it was a person who knew how to talk to a cat.

So Flutters got up and came over to Tim and put one paw up on his knee. She looked at him again for a moment and then she jumped up on his lap. She climbed up against his chest and put one paw against his cheek. And then she began to purr.

If she had met him in her own apartment, she wouldn't have done this. She probably wouldn't have paid any attention to him at all, because there she would have had her own people. But here she didn't; for hours she hadn't had anything. She'd been chased by dogs, and other cats, and monsters, and boys who should have known better. And now she'd found somebody who was kind, and who spoke gently to her. She wanted to show she appreciated it.

At first, Tim was a little uneasy with Flutters on his lap. He had never had a cat sit on him before and, while he appreciated it, he couldn't help remembering how sharp the cat's claws had been when she scratched George and how sharp her teeth had been when she bit Lenny. Now, the paw which touched Tim's cheek was as soft as velvet; Flutters wasn't showing any of her keen white teeth. But still—

Tim sat without moving for several minutes, and Flutters purred. Then Tim began to stroke her head. She purred harder than ever. She knew that things were all right, for the time being, and after a little Tim realized this too. It takes people longer to understand some things than it does cats.

They sat this way for about half an hour, and then Tim decided it was time to go back to the park and the ball game. He put Flutters down, and she stretched and looked at him to see what he was going to do next. He went to the door and she kept on looking at him. He said, "I'll be back, kitty," and went out and closed the door. And then Flutters began to cry—she was disappointed, and afraid again, and she said, "Ow-a-row-OO!" at the top of her voice. Tim started down the stairs, and he could still hear her. He stopped and listened, and Flutters cried harder than ever. So Tim went back. After all, he was responsible for the little cat. He couldn't get away from that.

He and Flutters were still in the apartment when Tim's father came home. Tim was lying on his cot, trying to read a book, and Flutters was lying on top of him, getting in his way. When Mr. Anderson opened the door, Flutters turned around, and sat up on Tim's chest, and stared at him. Now what? Flutters thought.

So did Mr. Anderson.

"What on earth?" Mr. Anderson said. When he spoke, Flutters jumped off Tim and went under Tim's cot. After a moment she looked out, showing just a dark face and wide blue eyes. She seemed to be listening to every word while Tim explained to his father how they happened to have a cat.

When Tim finished his father nodded, and said, "I don't see how you could have done anything else, son. But—" Then he looked at the face of the cat, sticking out from under the cot. Flutters stared at him, so Mr. Anderson said, "Hello," as was only polite. Flutters came part way out and said something in cat. Mr. Anderson held his left hand down so she could smell his fingers, and she came farther out and smelled them. Then she rubbed her head against his hand.

"She's a swell cat," Tim said. He didn't need to say he wanted to keep the little cat. Mr. Anderson looked at the boy, and at the cat, and thought Tim didn't have as much as most boys. But also he thought that food even for a little cat would cost money, and that he didn't have much money. It was hard enough to keep Tim dressed for school, and to keep the two of them fed, and pay the rent.

Then he looked at Tim again, and saw how much the boy wanted the little cat. And Flutters began to lick Mr. Anderson's hand with a small, rough tongue.

"Well, Tim," Mr. Anderson said, "we'll see what we can do."

CHAPTER TEN

Found:
One Siamese Cat

ON TUESDAY MORNING, AFTER TIM ANDERSON HAD GONE TO
school and Tim's father had gone out to see about a job a
man with only one good hand might be able to do, Flutters
lay curled up on Tim's cot. Since she had nothing better to
do at the moment, she went to sleep. And she dreamed.

Flutters was leading two lives by then, four days after she
had gone through an open door to see what was on the other
side. She led a life when she was awake, and it was all right.
She was beginning to be very fond of Tim, and she liked
his father, and she was learning to eat what they had to give
her. There wasn't much room to run around, so she slept a
good deal.

When she slept, she dreamed. She dreamed about Patty
and Howdy, and Mr. and Mrs. Burns. She dreamed about

the way they smelled and looked and even about the way, when she licked Patty's hand, Patty tasted. When she dreamed about them she would sometimes purr a little in her sleep, and sometimes she would make a small, strange noise, as if she were crying. That was her second life.

While Flutters slept, Patty Burns was on her way to school in a bus and she was thinking, "This is the day Flutters will come home." Howdy was on his way to his own school, and he was thinking that he guessed Flutters was lost for good. Mr. Burns was at his office, thinking mostly about business, and Mrs. Burns was calling up her sister, the children's Aunt Margaret, and saying that it looked as if they'd be asking for one of Diana's new kittens.

Tim's father was hearing a man say, "Sorry. Job's filled."

These things were all going on at the same time that Tuesday morning—Flutters dreaming, Patty telling herself over and over that, of *course*, they would find Flutters. Mr. Anderson not getting the job he needed, Mrs. Burns arranging for a kitten to take Flutters' place. Tim was thinking about his school work, because when you have a cat you don't have to keep thinking about it. It's when you've *lost* a cat that you think about it a lot.

And then, on his way home in the late afternoon, Mr. Anderson decided to stop in and get the pair of shoes he had left the day before to be half-soled. You wouldn't think that this had anything to do with what had been happening, but it had. If he had left his shoes at another shoemaker's, or gone in at a different time, the end of Flutters' adventure might have been quite different.

The shop he had left the shoes at was a little, dark shop, and it was cheap. That was why Mr. Anderson had taken his shoes there to be mended. He gave the shoemaker his ticket and paid him—in nickels and dimes and a few pennies —and the shoemaker wrapped the shoes up in a sheet of old newspaper. Mr. Anderson carried the shoes home under his arm. He said hello to Flutters. Tim wasn't home yet. He took off the shoes he had been wearing, which had holes in the bottoms, and put on the repaired shoes, which didn't. Then he picked up the newspaper in which the shoes had been wrapped and started to throw it in a wastebasket. Then he happened to notice it was the want-ad section. He started to look for "Help Wanted" advertisements and then saw that it was last Saturday morning's paper and started to throw it away again. Any jobs advertised in it would have been filled days ago.

He had crumpled the newspaper up and was about to toss it in the basket when he saw the advertisement. It was in the Lost and Found column, and Mr. Anderson read it first without really taking it in. Then he read it again:

"Lost: Young Siamese cat, seal-point female. Answers to the name of Flutters. Reward."

Tim and his father had decided to call Flutters "Leggins," because she wore them. Flutters had never paid any attention to that name.

Now Mr. Anderson said, "Flutters? Are you *Flutters?*"

The little cat jumped and turned around and looked at him. "Flutters?" Mr. Anderson said again. And then the little cat ran across the floor, and put both paws on Mr. Anderson's knees, and looked up into his face and began to talk—and talk and talk.

"Yes," Mr. Anderson said to the little cat, "I guess you are, all right."

Mr. Anderson got up, then, and went out of the apartment. He didn't have any telephone, but it wasn't a long walk. It was, Mr. Anderson thought as he went down the stairs, going to be tough on Tim. He was just as glad Tim hadn't been home when he found out. Of course, Tim would understand you can't keep somebody else's cat. Not when you know whose cat it is.

Although he needed badly any money he could get, Mr. Anderson wasn't thinking about the reward—just about Tim, and how much he would hate to give up the funny looking little cat.

It took Mr. Anderson about twenty minutes to walk to the apartment house the Burnses lived in. He walked across the park in which Tim had found Flutters. The park was a kind of dividing line between the apartment houses and the tenements. Once or twice, thinking about Tim, he almost turned back. Even when he was in the elevator, riding up to the Burns's apartment, he wanted to turn back. But he didn't. He rang the doorbell of the apartment.

Patty and Howdy were home from school and with their mother in the living room. Mrs. Burns was just getting ready to suggest they get a new kitten from Aunt Margaret and Diana when the bell rang. They heard Agnes going to answer it, and voices, and then Agnes came in.

"It's a man about that cat," Agnes said. She never could get over calling Flutters "that cat."

Patty and Howdy jumped up and hurried; Mrs. Burns, who had been disappointed a good many times before, followed them. They found a thin man, maybe about thirty-five years old, standing at the door. His suit wasn't new, and his shoes weren't. He stood up straight, but his right arm was bent at the elbow and his right hand was twisted. He said, "I think I've got the cat you advertised about."

Patty's face lighted up, and so did Howdy's. Mrs. Burns said she hoped he had, and invited him in. When he came in, he described the little cat his son had found, and told how she had acted when he asked her if she was Flutters. Patty jumped up and down, or almost did, because this time it really *was* Flutters. Howdy said, *"Gee!"* Mr. Anderson said he hadn't brought Flutters with him because he had nothing to carry her in, and was afraid if he tried to carry her in his arms she would be frightened, and run away again.

Then Mr. Burns came home. "Dad!" Howdy said; Howdy almost shouted. "He's found Flutters!" He pointed to Mr. Anderson.

"We're just going over to Mr. Anderson's house to get

her," Patty said, and ran to get the carrying box in which they had first brought Flutters from the country. Then everything seemed to be happening at once. Patty and Howdy and Mr. and Mrs. Burns—everybody—went to get Flutters and bring her home.

As they walked across the park, Mr. Anderson and Mr. Burns walked together, and Mr. Anderson said that his son, Tim, was going to hate losing the cat. And then, because Mr. Burns was interested, Tim's father told him about how little Tim had, and how it had happened, and how he had saved the little cat—told him about everything. Mr. Anderson hadn't talked so much about himself and Tim for a long time; he did now, as they walked, because Mr. Burns seemed to be interested. He even told Mr. Burns how he had learned to keep books.

Tim had just got home when they all reached the Anderson's apartment. He was down on his knees, talking to Flutters, and rubbing behind her ears. Then his father came in, with the others, and Tim saw that the strange man—who was Mr. Burns, of course—was carrying a black, oblong box with a handle in the top. He knew, of course, what had happened. Anyone would have known. He stood up and looked at all of them and then he just said, "Oh," in a strange, flat voice.

But Patty was down on her knees by that time, saying "Flutters. Oh—Flutters!" And Flutters, who had already

been purring because Tim was stroking her—well, Flutters acted like a crazy cat.

She ran to Patty, first, and seemed to climb all over her. At the same time, Flutters talked, and she sounded angry, or almost angry. She was scolding Patty for having been gone so long—it was as if Patty, not Flutters, had been the one who had run away and caused all the trouble.

Then Flutters went to Howdy and did the same thing, and then to Mrs. Burns and then to Mr. Burns. Then she went back to Patty again. Then she did it all over. No one had ever seen a more excited little cat.

Tim just watched. There wasn't anything to say or do. Mr. Anderson stood by his son, and put his arm around the boy's shoulders, but there wasn't anything to say.

At the last minute, just before she was put in the box, Flutters went over to Tim and spoke to him, and then to Mr. Anderson. Probably she was saying "Thank you." But she didn't waste time on it. She ran back to Patty. And then she was in the box.

Mr. Burns motioned with his head to Mrs. Burns, and she said, "Come on, Patty, Howdy." The three of them, Howdy carrying Flutters in the box, went down the stairs and crossed the street and started through the park. They were almost across it when Mr. Burns caught up with them. Then he and Mrs. Burns walked on ahead, talking. Neither Patty nor Howdy was much interested in what their father and mother were talking about. They were interested in Flutters, who was moving around inside the box and yelling. They kept talking to her, and telling her she was going home.

Only once or twice, on the walk home, did Patty think about Tim, and the way he had said "Oh" in that disappointed voice, when he realized he was going to lose Flutters. She was too excited at having Flutters back to think about much else.

It was only later—after Flutters had smelled the whole apartment to make sure she was really home, and sat on everybody's lap, and had a large dinner and gone to sleep on a sofa where she wasn't supposed to—that Patty and Howdy began to think about Tim, and how unhappy he must be. It was after they had their own dinner that they talked about it together and then talked to their father and mother.

"I'll bet he misses her like—like anything," Howdy said, and Patty said, "Couldn't we do something?"

Mr. and Mrs. Burns looked at each other, and Mrs. Burns smiled and nodded to her husband, and he nodded back.

But all Mr. Burns said was, "We'll see," and all Mrs. Burns said was that it was time Patty and Howdy did their home work.

So what happened the next day was a complete surprise.

CHAPTER ELEVEN

The Good Luck Cat

FLUTTERS WAS UP BRIGHT AND EARLY WEDNESDAY MORN-
ing. She had dreamed during the night that being home
was all a dream, so as soon as she woke up she had to go all
over the apartment and smell everything to be sure. Everything smelled fine to Flutters. Flutters felt fine. She wanted
to share how she felt with her people, so she went to the
door of Patty's room and talked through it, and scratched it.
Then she went to Howdy's door and then to the door of Mr.
and Mrs. Burns's room. Everywhere she went she said, "I'm
here! I'm home! Wake up!" Everybody did wake up, too.
When a Siamese cat says something, you hear it. Patty let
Flutters in, and Flutters jumped up on Patty's bed and
walked back and forth, purring. Now and then she stopped
long enough to lick Patty's face.

82

After a while, Patty got up and dressed for school, stopping now and then to pet Flutters—and to get Flutters to let go of things she wanted to play with, like stockings. By the time Patty was dressed, the others were up, too. But Mr. Burns wasn't dressed for his office. He was dressed in the things he wore when they drove out into the country for a day. And so was Mrs. Burns. It was Mrs. Burns who told Patty and Howdy that they weren't going to school that day; that they were going out to see Aunt Margaret and, of course, the proud cat, Diana.

"But—" Howdy said. "Won't we miss things at school? I mean—"

It wasn't that he didn't look forward to a drive in the country instead of school, as anybody would. But he had learned that school is important, and not to be missed without a really important reason.

"I telephoned your teacher last night, Howdy," Mrs. Burns said. "Yours too, Patty. It'll be all right, this once."

That made it all right; that made it wonderful. Both Patty and Howdy changed from their school clothes into clothes they wore in the country, and right after breakfast, Mr. Burns said he would go around to the garage and get the car.

He telephoned up from downstairs in about twenty minutes and they all went down—except Flutters, who was staying at home. She had had breakfast and had gone back to sleep, anyway, and didn't seem to mind. She was used to people going out and coming back; already, here where she belonged, she was beginning to forget she had ever been away. She would have preferred all the Burnses to stay at home with her, but if they didn't she would wait until they came back. She had a good deal of sleep to catch up on, of course.

Before the Burnses went, they made Agnes promise to be very careful about open doors. Agnes said she certainly would. And before they went, Mrs. Burns got Flutters' carrying box out of the storage closet. When Howdy and Patty asked why, their mother said they would see, soon enough.

When they got down to the car in front of the apartment house, their father was in it—and Tim Anderson and Mr. Anderson were in it too. Patty and Howdy both said "Good morning" to Mr. Anderson and "Hi" to Tim. Tim said " 'lo." Neither Mr. Anderson nor Tim was dressed for the country, particularly. Mr. Anderson wore the suit he had worn the afternoon before, because it was the only suit he had—the only one that wasn't completely worn out.

It was a beautiful spring morning in the country. There seemed to be pink and white dogwood everywhere; it was warm enough to have the car windows open, and they could all hear birds singing. Tim looked this way and that way, as if he had never seen anything like this before—and as a matter of fact, he never had. Oh, he had been in city parks and all that, but not really in the country. The country made

him forget, a little, about losing Flutters, although he still kept thinking of her. It had been lonely the night before with no small cat snuggled against him.

He didn't know any more than Patty and Howdy did what the trip was all about. Oh, they guessed, of course. Patty and Howdy were pretty sure; Tim just knew it was *something*—probably part of the reward for finding Flutters.

They reached Aunt Margaret's house in about an hour and drove up to the circle in front of the porch. And there, on the porch, were five Siamese cats, sitting in a row. They all sat the same way, with their tails wrapped around them and the tips resting on their forepaws, the way proper cats sit. Four of the cats were still kittens, and two of them sat on either side of the larger cat, who was Diana. She was prouder at that moment than she had ever been in her life— *four* beautiful kittens!

The five cats watched the car stop, and the kittens looked at Diana to see what she did. If she ran, they would run. But Diana didn't run. It had been some time since she had seen Patty and Howdy, and a long time since she had made friends with them. But she hadn't forgotten them. She knew they were all right for cats, and she told the kittens so. Anybody they brought along, Diana told the kittens, would be all right, too.

Aunt Margaret came out and met Tim and Mr. Anderson, and suggested they all go around to the back yard. They all did, and Diana and her kittens went too—Diana first and the kittens following in single file, like a cat parade. In the yard, the grown people sat down and talked and Patty and Howdy and Tim got acquainted with the kittens and Patty and Howdy got acquainted with Tim. Diana played for a while, too, but then she sat on Aunt Margaret's lap and watched, and listened to the conversation. She was a grown-up cat, of course.

The kittens looked almost exactly alike, as Siamese cats do. They looked like Diana, and they looked like Flutters. They acted pretty much alike, but as you watched them you began to be able to tell them apart. There was one who seemed to start most of the games, and one who had a habit of running part way up an old apple tree and then backing down, and one who always rolled over on his back when he was pretending to fight with his brothers and sisters. Two of the kittens were males and two were females, incidentally.

And the one who started most of the games took a special liking to Tim. Cats do that; pick out special people. Nobody knows why, except cats. This kitten just decided that Tim was the best of the people around, that day in the back yard in the country.

They all had lunch after a while, including the cats, who got nibbles of this and that, and after lunch, the grownups looked at one another, and Aunt Margaret nodded and then Mr. Anderson said:

"Well, Tim, which one will it be?"

Tim just looked at his father; just looked and his face

lighted up. He'd hoped, of course. But still—

"To take home, son," Mr. Anderson said. "Thanks to—"
He didn't finish; if he hadn't been a grown man, you would
have thought he choked up a little.

"Gee!" Tim said. "Oh—*gee*, Dad!"

There wasn't any doubt which kitten Tim would take
home. The kitten had decided that already—the kitten who
always seemed to start the games. Usually, in situations like
that, a person can leave it to the cat.

The kitten—it hadn't any name yet, or no real name; just
a temporary name—had to ride back to the city in the carrying box. She didn't like it, and said so. Tim held the box
on his knees and talked to the kitten through the grating in
the front. The kitten talked back, mostly at the top of her
voice. She sounded very much like Flutters.

Mr. Burns drove them all to the door of the tenement
building Tim and his father lived in. Mr. Anderson got out
first, and held the kitten in the box while Tim got out. Tim
said goodbye to everybody, but he wanted to hurry upstairs
and let his kitten out, and give her some milk.

Mr. Anderson hesitated a moment. He started to say
something, and stopped.

"Skip it," Mr. Burns said, and grinned at him.

"I can't do that," Mr. Anderson said. "This chance you're
giving me at a job. Tim's kitten. The whole business.
It's—"

"Sure," Mr. Burns said. "You're due for a little luck.

You and the kid. And, as I said, we need a bookkeeper."

Both of them sounded a little gruff about it, to Patty and Howdy. But grown people are like that, sometimes.

"Well," Mr. Anderson said, "Flutters brought us luck, all right. She's a good luck cat."

The Burnses went home, after that. Flutters met them at the door, all caught up on her sleep. Patty picked her up; Patty looked around the comfortable place they all lived in.

"You know," Patty said to Flutters, "you're a lucky cat."

Flutters purred.